Adventures with MALAKAi

TEAMWORK MAKES THE DREAM WORK

Written by
Malakai Roberts
&
Percy Miller

ISBN: 979-8-88896-076-9

First Edition
10 9 8 7 6 5 4 3 2 1

Printed in USA

ADVENTURES WITH MALAKAI
TEAMWORK MAKES THE DREAM WORK

Written by
Malakai Roberts & Percy Miller

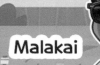

Malakai

Uncle P

Captain Ace

One sunny afternoon,
Malakai, **Uncle P**, **Max** and **Roxy** were
finishing their bowls of **Snoop Loopz**
on a picnic table.

Malakai says, "Thanks for a **delicious**
breakfast, Unc. Now I'm ready
to train."

Uncle P says, "You're welcome. Have a great
training day with the **K-9 Team**. Are you guys
playing basketball today?

Malakai replies, "No basketball today but we
will be doing a variety of things."

Uncle P replies, "Ok Malakai, remember that you are **special**. Even though you **lost** your eyesight, you can still do so many things like ride a bike, which I am still learning how to do. So have fun with your friends, **teamwork** makes the dream work. I'll see you afterwards."

Malakai, Max and Roxy
wave goodbye to Uncle P and head off to
training at their karate class with the
Great Master Coach Panda.

"Hi-Yah!" Roxy exclaimed
as she executed a roundhouse
kick in the air.

"Hee-Agh!"
Max grunted as he performed a
spinning back kick.

Great Master Coach Panda
says, "Ok Malakai, it's your
turn to kick."

Malakai jump kicks
in the air but **slips** and lands
on his bottom.

5

Roxy and Max rush to help him up.
Max asks, "Are you okay?" Roxy says, "Don't worry,
Malakai. The more you practice the **better**
you'll be able to kick."

Malakai gets up and dusts himself off.

Malakai, Max and Roxy
continue training with Great Master Coach
Panda punching and doing footwork
with **enthusiasm**.

Great Master Coach Panda **announces**, "I need
everyone's full attention."

The students immediately
stopped what they were doing
and stood at attention to listen.
Great Master Coach Panda continued,
"We will end training with a test.
In order to **graduate** to the next
karate belt, you **must** break
this piece of wood."

Great Master Coach Panda
gives an example chopping a piece
of wood in two, with his **pinky** and a
calm face, then says, "Now you try."

The students break the
wood one by one.

Roxy cracks her knuckles,
jumps in the air landing with a hand chop
breaking the wood. Everyone claps.

Max walks up to the piece of wood and uses
his elbow with quick **force** to break it in half.
Everyone claps again.

"Malakai, are you ready? It's your turn," said
Great Master Coach Panda.

Malakai takes a huge gulp and nervously
steps up.

Malakai whispers to encourage himself, "If
Roxy and Max can do it, so can I."

Malakai hand chops the wood with **all** of his
might but it doesn't budge or break.

Malakai looks **defeated** and says,
"You know what? I'm no good at karate.
I think I'm going to see what Hercules
is doing and join him!"

Malakai joins
Hercules at the pool.

"Let's swim some laps in the pool,"
Hercules exclaims.

"I **love** to swim, replied Malakai, "this is going
to be easy, way **better** than karate."

They both put on goggles and swam
across the pool eagerly.

Malakai shouts,

"Woohoo! This is **fun**!"

Hercules initiates
the next activity and
says, "Now, it's time for
weightlifting."

Hercules benches a
heavyweight barbell.

Malakai takes a breath and
attempts to lift the weight but struggles.

"Unhhhhh, come on!"

Malakai **can't** pick up the weight. Hercules
says, "Here, let me **help** you."

Malakai replies, "No, it's ok.
I'm going to see what Captain Ace
is doing," as he jets out of

the door.

14

Malakai joins **Captain Ace** on the track field with the track team. Malakai and Captain Ace have fun long jumping.

"Now this is more like it!" says Malakai. Then, he and Captain Ace jump on the trampoline.

"This is much **better** than karate and lifting weights," Malakai tells Captain Ace.

Captain Ace laughs, "Why don't we run a few laps!"

Malakai agrees, "Ok! Let's do it!"

The track team begins running.

They run one lap.

"How are you holding up?"
Captain Ace asks Malakai.

"I'm feeling **great!**" replies Malakai.

16

They run **two** laps.

By lap three, Malakai is **sweating** profusely and is exhausted.

Captain Ace announces to the team, "We've got five more laps left team!"

Malakai smiles at Captain Ace trying to hold it together but he becomes breathless and **faints**.

Malakai walks off of the field **disappointed** and sits on a bench. He holds his head down.

Captain Ace runs over to his **friend** Malakai and sits next to him on the bench.

Captain Ace asks, "What's the matter, Malakai?"

Malakai replies, "I'm **sad**."

Captain Ace asks, "Why?"

Malakai says, " I'm **not** good at karate like Roxy and Max. I'm not good at lifting weights like Hercules. And I'm not good at running like you, Captain Ace."

Malakai covers his face holding back tears.

Malakai sobs, " I'm not good at **anything**!"

Captain Ace says, "That's not true at all, Malakai. You're good at **plenty** of things. You can ride a bike. You can build a robot! You're great at reading, studying and figuring out solutions to problems."

Uncle P, Hercules, Max and Roxy walk over to join Malakai and Captain Ace on the bench.

Hercules says,
"You put others **before** yourself.
And you make the **best** grilled
cheese sandwich!"

Roxy says, "You know **a lot** about animals and
you helped me get an A+ on my Math test. I
would've never passed without **your** help!"

Max says, "You have a **strong** sense of smell and
touch. You taught me to dribble the basketball
and told me to never give up or quit even when
things seem hard."

Uncle P says, "You are **fearless**. You love and
care about your family. You're kind, thoughtful
and care about others. Those are the best
qualities to have. You are a **champion!**"

Captain Ace says, "And most importantly, you're
a **good** friend. You are always ready to **help**
the team and **anyone** in need."

Malakai **smiles**, "Well, I
guess when you guys put it that way,
I'm good at some things."

Captain Ace says, "**God** made us all **different**.
No matter what our limitations are, nobody is
perfect. We're not all supposed to be good at
the same things. But when we all put our
strengths **together**, that's what makes
us a great team."

Max says, "There is no 'I' in team."

Roxy has a great idea, she says, " Hey, speaking
of **team**..."

Roxy holds out her fist. Hercules, Captain Ace,
Max, Malakai and Uncle P bump their fists
together in a team **handshake**.